A WEEK WITH

MOM

A WEEK WITH MOM

MOM

A Play in One Act

By

Jan Yager

Hannacroix Creek Books, Inc.

Stamford, Connecticut

Please address performance inquiries to the publisher: Hannacroix Creek Books, Inc. (hannacroix@aol.com)

Published by:
Hannacroix Creek Books, Inc.
https://www.hannacroixcreekbooks.com
hannacroix@aol.com

ISBN: 978-1-938998-33-1 (trade paperback)

Contents

A WEEK WITH MOM
A ONE-ACT PLAY

Scene 1

Hotel Registration Desk, London, England, Morning

MRS. SANDRA ACKER, *81, looks fabulous for her age. You would think she is in her late 50s or early 60s. She's beautiful, with an excellent figure, and she's wearing black leggings and dressed like she's very mod for her age. Her hair is brown and not too short and not too long. She's wearing interesting costume jewelry that adds to her mod look. She looks at the empty reception desk and then looks at her daughter,*

LIDIA MILLER, *56, is beautiful but in a much less dramatic way than her mother. Prematurely gray, she dies her hair, so she is also a brunette. Her outfit is much more business casual than glamorous, but she still makes an impressive appearance. It is hard for Mrs. Acker to hide her obvious displeasure that they are being kept waiting.*

MRS. ACKER

This place is a dump.

LIDIA

Mother, you haven't even seen your room yet.

MRS. ACKER

But look at this lobby? I thought we'd be staying in a
luxury hotel.

LIDIA

Remember, Mother, this trip is my treat. I'm so sorry
I couldn't afford a couple of hundred pounds a night
at a more luxurious hotel. But this hotel is affordable.

I am so sorry you're disappointed.

*MRS. ACKER takes another long look at the lobby. It
is one of those modest hotels converted out of a private
home in a row of townhouses that are now all hotels.
It is near the Underground and near to the convention
center which makes it a favorite hotel for those who
are on a more modest travel budget.*

MRS. ACKER

How long are we staying?

LIDIA

A week.

MRS. ACKER

And the whole time we'll be at this hotel?

LIDIA

I apologize that you have such a negative feeling
about this hotel.

MRS. ACKER

We're staying a whole week? Do you mean seven
days or five days?

LIDIA

Mom, you remind me of Dad. He would ask when he
could leave as soon as you both arrived for a visit.

MRS. ACKER

Raising her voice.

8

Don't you say anything bad about your father, may
his soul rest in peace.

LIDIA

All I'm saying is that I want you to enjoy this trip.
Don't focus on how long we'll be here. Focus on
spending a week in London with your daughter. And
it's not even costing you a dime.

MRS. ACKER

I would have gladly paid for the hotel if I knew you
were going to put us up in a dump like this.

LIDIA

One of my colleagues in publishing recommended
this hotel. She stays here every year when she attends
the Book Fair.

MRS. ACKER

Who is this friend or colleague of yours who
recommended this place? I don't think I've ever hear

you mention her before. And you took her word for
it?

LIDIA

Once again, I apologize for disappointing you. Can
you at least wait to pass judgment till you see your
room?

MRS. ACKER

If this is what the lobby is like, I don't hold out
much hope for what my room is going to be like.
I'm hoping it at least doesn't have bed bugs.

LIDIA

The hotel looks very nice at their website and my
colleague has always found it a positive experience.
She said their breakfasts are delicious. Very British.

MRS. ACKER

Not really a concern of mine. Breakfast. I thought you'd be getting us rooms at one of the luxury hotels. Even one of the American chains but their London version.

LIDIA

That would have costs hundreds of pounds or dollars. Mother, this is London, Mother. They have different standards here. This is actually considered a very nice moderately-price hotel that is a favorite with business travelers.

MRS ACKER

But I'm not here on business.

LIDIA

I am, and remember, the reason you agreed to go on this trip with me is because I told you I needed your help to staff my stand at the London Book Fair.

MRS. ACKER

That's right. I want you to have a success with your company and that's why I agreed to go on this trip.

LIDIA

So let's just check in and make the most of it, okay?

MRS. ACKER

Reluctantly she answers.

If you say so.

Blackout.

Scene II

Lidia's room in the hotel. It's several hours later and they've had lunch at a restaurant around the corner from the hotel.

MRS. ACKER

I'm stuffed.

LIDIA

You barely ate anything at lunch.

MRS. ACKER

Just because I didn't finish everything on my plate doesn't mean that I didn't have a substantial lunch. You could take a hint from me, and you'd never have a weight problem. Besides, I didn't really like the food. My salad was quite bland and the bread was somewhat stale.

LIDIA

I'm so sorry you didn't like the food.

MRS. ACKER

That's okay. The restaurant matches this hotel.

LIDIA

I'm really sorry the trip is such a disappointment so far, Mother.

MRS. ACKER

Well at least I could stay on my diet at lunch. So many people complain that they gain weight when they travel.

LIDIA

Mother, could we avoid the topic of weight for just one day? You've been harping on my weight since I'm ten years old. Let's just enjoy each other's company and our trip.

MRS. ACKER

Reluctantly

I'll try.

There is an awkward silence for a few seconds.

What did my grandson Mark say to you as he and your husband were leaving you at the airport? I couldn't hear Mark, but I saw whatever he said to you made quite an impression on you. I know you replied something back and he seemed to think long and hard about what you said to him.

LIDIA

It was nothing, Mother.

MRS. ACKER

Nothing? Now I know it was something or you'd tell me right away.

LIDIA

It's not a big deal.

MRS. ACKER

So, if it's not a big deal, just tell me already.

LIDIA

Okay. Mark asked me why I was going on a trip to London with his grandmother at my age.

MRS. ACKER

So, what did you reply.

LIDIA

I said I'm going to London for a week with my mother, your grandmother, at 56 because I never spent time with her when I was his age. I reassured him that he wouldn't have to go on a trip with me when he's 56 because he and I have been spending time together throughout his childhood.

Mrs. Acker almost instantly gets visibly angry and upset but she stops herself from having any kind of an outburst. Instead, she resorts to sarcasm.

MRS. ACKER

Well, isn't that special. Well, aren't you the perfect
mother.

LIDIA

No, Mother, I'm certainly not perfect. I wasn't
bragging. I was just telling you what Mark said
because you asked.

MRS. ACKER

What does my grandson Mark know anyway? What
is he twelve? thirteen years old?

LIDIA

He's fifteen, Mother.

MRS. ACKER

*She takes a deep breath before she blurts out her next
pronouncement*

Lidia, all I know is that *you* had a happy childhood.

LIDIA

Mother, I must tell *you* that I had a happy childhood.
You can't tell *me* that I had a happy childhood.

MRS. ACKER

Repeating her comment as if she is oblivious to her
daughter's response and in a more adamant tone.

No, I was there and I know that *you* had a happy
childhood.

LIDIA

Mother, I'm going to say it again. *I* must be the one
to tell *you* that my childhood was happy. You just
can't tell someone that.

MRS. ACKER

So you've never told Mark that he's had a happy
childhood?

LIDIA

I don't have to.

MRS. ACKER

Why's that?

LIDIA

*Answering somewhat cautiously, fearful of the
response her words may get.*
Because Mark often tells me —volunteers —that he's
happy and that he's been having a wonderful
childhood.

MRS. ACKER

I don't believe you. You're making it up to hurt me.

LIDIA

I'm sorry if you think that I'm making it up to hurt
you. You know we're not in competition, Mother.

MRS. ACKER

Whatever. Let's switch the subject.

LIDIA

Good idea. So, if we're not going to talk about my weight, or whether or not I had a happy childhood, what do you want to talk about?

MRS. ACKER

I'm glad you asked me to help out at the London Book Fair where they speak English. I don't think I'd feel comfortable where I don't speak or understand the language, like France or Italy.

LIDIA

I bet you'd do better than you think you would do. Maybe we could go to either or both of those countries next.

MRS. ACKER

Let's see how this trip goes before we start planning the next one. It's only been a day.

LIDIA

Closer to two days if you count the overnight flight
as a day.

There are several seconds of silence, as it becomes
clear that both are becoming increasingly
uncomfortable by the silence. It is the silence of two
people who have little in common and don't talk
to each other often enough to have small talk that
they can easily share with each other. It's the
silence of a mother and daughter who are trying to
put into a week the closeness they hadn't felt for
many decades. The awkwardness that each feels
being around each other is quite obvious.

MRS. ACKER
Eager to change the subject and to switch to
something more neutral..
Do you realize it's been raining since we arrived?
Talking at the same time as LIDIA

LIDIA

Rains a lot here, doesn't it?

Lidia stops herself from laughing as she realized they
were both reduced to talking about the weather.

MRS. ACKER

I wish your father was on this trip with us.

LIDIA

Lidia takes a deep breath as she holds back her tears.

Mother, Dad's been gone nine years now.

MRS. ACKER

I know.

LIDIA

And you even got engaged to that doctor you

met through the tennis group you belonged to.

Dr. Blair Blau. I was sorry when he died but

you picked someone after Dad who was even

older than you than Dad was. Dad was only

seven years older, but Dr. Blair was ten years older.

MRS. ACKER

Yes, Dr. Blair Blau. We had four good years together. It was so sad when he died.

LIDIA

I was sad too, Mom, and I even went to the funeral even though Dr. Blau told me and my sister that he didn't want to get to know us because he just wanted to spend whatever time he had left enjoying his relationship with you.

MRS. ACKER

That makes sense. Can you blame him?

LIDIA

Yes! It was a cruel thing to say to me and my sister Pat. We wanted to get to know him and enjoy

spending time together as a family. What he said hurt
our feelings.

MRS. ACKER

That's ridiculous! Maybe you'll understand what he
meant more when you get to be 91.

LIDIA

I don't think getting older is an excuse for being cruel
in what you say. I know people say that about old
people, but I don't give anyone a pass, whatever their
age.

MRS ACKER

It's easy for you to say at 56. Just wait till you get to
81 like me.

LIDIA

That reminds me of another cruel thing Dr. Blair said.
He was bragging one time, before you got engaged so

he was still willing to spend time around me and my family, and you were bragging about how many people are shocked when you tell them your age. I think you were 78 or 79 at the time. You or boyfriend Dr. Blair looked you straight in the eye and he said, "Someday you'll say that, and no one will be shocked by your age because you'll look your age." I thought that was very cruel to say that.

MRS. ACKER

You're lying! I don't remember Dr. Blair saying any such thing!

LIDIA

Why would I lie about something like that?

MRS. ACKER

To hurt my feelings.

LIDIA

That's the last thing I'd ever want to do. I do love you, mother.

MRS. ACKER

Well, you have a strange way of showing it! Saying such lies about my fiancé whom I miss very much.

LIDIA

I know you miss him but I'm not making it up.

MRS. ACKER

If he was alive, if your father was alive, I wouldn't be on this trip with you.

LIDIA

Now that's absolutely true! I know you're on this trip to help me out with my stand at the Book Fair but I also think it's because you're in between husbands or fiancés.

Mrs. Acker slaps Lidia across the face.
There is a new silence in the room as Lidia waits for her mother to apologize.

MRS. ACKER

Take it back.

LIDIA

Take back what I said even though it's the truth?
How about you take back slapping me across the
face.

MRS. ACKER

No, because you deserved it.

LIDIA

Mother, I'm not six years old and a little kid
that you can hit with a strap as you screamed
out, "Wait till your father gets home," as you
hit me across the butt but when Dad got home,
he never did anything to discipline me. It was
always you.

MRS. ACKER

Never happened.

LIDIA

Are you calling me a liar?

MRS. ACKER

Yes. I never hit you. Never once in your entire
childhood.

LIDIA

Yes, you did.

MRS ACKER

Liar liar pants on fire!

LIDIA

Okay. I'll prove it.

She goes to the phone in the room and picks it up.

Thank you, operator. I want to make a long-distance
call to Boston, Massachusetts. Collect. (Pause) Yes,
I'll put in the number.

(pause)

Okay. I'll hold.

Pause

Thank you.

Lidia now speaks to her sister on the phone but only the audience or Mrs. Acker hears Lidia's comments. But we can tell from what she is saying that her sister is confirming her memories of their childhood.

Sis, I'm here in London with Mom. You know that business trip we went on together. (pause) Yes, we're getting along, sort of. (pause) What have we been doing so far? We arrived this morning and we unpacked. Then we went out to lunch and walked around the neighborhood. Then we went out to dinner, also in the neighborhood. (pause) No, we have two separate rooms. I thought that was a better idea. (pause) Sis, the reason I called is I wanted to ask you to verify that Mom used a strap or what they today call a belt on us when she got mad at us when we were growing up. (pause) Okay, you confirm that I'm right. (pause) Let

29

me ask her if she wants me to put her on the phone.

Mom, do you want to talk to my sister to hear her confirmation?

Mrs. Acker shakes her head no.

No, that's okay, Sis. That won't be necessary. Listen, this is costing you a fortune because I called collect so I'm going to hang up now. Love you. Hope to get together soon. Let me know when you're coming down from Boston next, closer to Westchester, and I'll let you know when I can get up there.

Lidia hangs up the phone.

There, Mother, confirmation from my sister.

MRS. ACKER

Your sister's lying. I never thought she was a liar like you. But she is. I can't believe it. My two daughters making up stories about me and their childhood.

LIDIA

It happened, Mother, even if you don't want to own up to it. You took a strap to us. You traumatized me. You traumatized my sister. Yes, I had some happy moments during my childhood, but I wouldn't say I had a happy childhood.

MRS. ACKER

I want to go home.

Lidia takes a deep breath.

LIDIA

I never stood up to you when I was a child. I wish I had. I think you didn't know any better. Grandma took a strap to you. Or your father or your older brother. But it made me very sad as a kid.

MRS. ACKER

I want to go home.

Lidia took another deep breath, and she takes a few moments to think. She's obviously weighing her options. Does she apologize to her mother? Does she beg her to stay and work things out with her? What should she do?

LIDIA

In a much louder voice as she is visibly shaking.

I'm not a little girl that you can abuse!

MRS. ACKER

Keep your voice down! They might hear what we're talking about!

LIDIA

The tears are streaming down her face now.

I can 't believe it, Mother. You're more concerned about total strangers in a hotel in London far away from anyone that you know hearing what we're talking about than the pain you caused me during my formative years. How I wish you could understand what it was like to be so afraid of my mother not just as a child but even as an adult. Never standing up to you. Always being afraid you might withhold or withdraw your love if I expressed how I felt. You were the Queen of the silence treatment. I think the silent treatment which I know could even go on for weeks not just hours or days was even crueler than the physical hits with the belt

MRS. ACKER

Stop talking about the past! Stop talking about ancient history! You're trying to make me feel awful.

Haven't I suffered enough in my lifetime? My father's death when I was just nineteen. Your father's death and he didn't even have life insurance because he didn't believe in it. Your brother's death. My mother's death. My two first cousins who died during World War II.

LIDIA

I know you've had a lot of loss but that doesn't give
you the right to hit your children or to give your
daughter the silent treatment.

MRS. ACKER

I knew this trip was a bad idea. I knew spending time
with you would be a nightmare. I want to go home.

*Lidia wipes her tears away and takes a deep breath
as she picks up the phone.*

If that's what you want to do, that's fine. I'll call you
a taxi.

*Mrs. Acker almost falls on the bed she is so startled
by her daughter's response. It was not what she
expected to hear. It was a big change from what her
daughter had always done before. Placating her.
Compromising. Asking to make up with her.
Silence for several seconds as Mrs. Acker weighs her
options.*

No, that's okay.

LIDIA

Are you sure? Because I'm happy to call you a cab.

MRS. ACKER

No, I'll stay.

LIDIA

One more thing. You never hug me. You never have.

MRS. ACKER

There is a silence and then Mrs. Acker starts to cry

ever so softly.

And I never will.

(pause)

My mother never hugged me.

LIDIA

There is another pause and silence and then Lidia
walks over to her mother who initially pulls back
because she doesn't know what to expect from her
daughter, fearing her daughter might slap her the way
she did earlier.

Lidia slaps her mother. This time it's even harder than the first slap.

LIDIA

Sorry, mother. I need to victimize you the way you victimized me when I was too little to fight back.

MRS. ACKER

(Starting to cry)
Please stop, Lidia.

LIDIA

She slaps her mother, even harder.
Sorry. I'd like to stop, but I can't.

MRS. ACKER

When I mistreated you as an infant and toddler, I didn't know any better, Lidia. But you know better. You're a mature woman. You have a family of your own.

LIDIA

I know I'm 56 years old but I'm actually still that child inside that you abused.

MRS. ACKER *cries even louder. As she cries louder, Lidia takes a knife off of a tray that had the remnants of their earlier snack of tea and crumpets.*

MRS. ACKER

Her eyes are widened with fear.

Lidia, you're not going to use that knife, are you? How will you explain it to the authorities if you stab me or worse? You could go to prison in a foreign country. Stop this nonsense, this torture, now!

LIDIA

I've already thought that through, mother. I plan to stab myself, but not fatally,

and I'll tell that that *you* attacked me and I
was defending myself!

MRS. ACKER

You think they'll believe you?

LIDIA

Why not? Countless killers get away
with it every day by claiming self-defense.

MRS. ACKER

She is crying even louder now.

I'm so sorry that I mistreated you as
a baby.

LIDIA

Putting the knife to her mother's
throat.

Say that louder, mother!

MRS. ACKER

Okay. I'm so sorry that I was a selfish mother and that I brutalized you when you were little.

Mrs. Acker says it in a very loud voice.

She is visibly shaking and the fear in her eyes is like a deer in headlights as a car is about to barrel into it.

Suddenly, Lidia takes the knife away. She puts it down as she takes a deep breath. She walks over to the sink in the hotel room and throws cold water on her face.

LIDIA

Say that again, mother!

MRS. ACKER

I'm so sorry!

LIDIA

I never understood the reason the Menendez brothers killed their mother and father who allegedly abused them during their childhood. I always used to say, 'Why didn't they just run away? They were 18 and 21 when the killings occurred. They were old enough and rich enough to get on a plane and go to another country and begin a new life. They never had to see their parents again.

But today I came in touch with the rage that they must of both felt. The normal childhood and teen years that they were denied because of what their parents allegedly did to them.

I almost fell into that trap myself. I almost stabbed you, mother. I might have killed you.

Lidia goes over to her mother who is still frightened that her daughter is going to stab or kill her. Instead, Lidia gives her mother a big hug as her mother just stands there, almost limp, not knowing how to respond. But her mother doesn't push her away, yet she doesn't hug her back either.

Thank you for sharing, mother, that you were victimized by your mother and brother. You were just passing on to me what was done to you. Fortunately, the abuse stopped with me. I had not done to my family what you did to me. Well then. I'll just have to hug *you*. But remember always that you had a choice. To pass along the abuse or to go in a different direction. Saying you're sorry helps a little but it won't cancel out my memories of being scalded with hot coffee when I was still in a high chair or being ignored at two so that I walked into a wall and have a scar on my forehead. Or you accusing me of trying to turn on my father when I was a preteen. And so many other physical and emotional traumas. The name calling, for example.

MRS. ACKER

Weeping as her past atrocities toward her daughter are painstakingly detailed.

I'll say "sorry" again

Lidia now squeezes her mother even tighter. They stand there, awkwardly, for a few moments as Lidia holds on to her mother who is not pushing her away but not hugging her bag either.

MRS. ACKER

(She speaks to her daughter, her voice almost cracking as she fights back her

emotion, after a few moments of

awkwardness)

Okay, young lady. Now that we've both let our hair down, I think it's time for us to see what all the fuss is about since I haven't been to London in decades. You know your father and I got to London but that was more than twenty years ago. Let's take a taxi or get on one of those double decker buses that are one of my favorite memories of London and head down to Piccadilly Circus where all the tourists go. Maybe we can even get some theater tickets for later in the week.

LIDIA

That sounds like a great idea, Mom! Let me give my husband and Mark a quick phone call to let them know how the trip's going, and then we can head out for a night on the town.

MRS. ACKER

(Still somewhat shaky as she realizes she came so close to being stabbed by her daughter.)

No big deal. Besides, it costs more if you buy it at the last minute and I really didn't want to buy myself a new airline ticket.

Lidia is about to comment on her mother's response but she decides to let the comment go.

Blackout

About the Author

Jan Yager, the former J.L. (Janet Lee) Barkas, grew up in Bayside, Queens, New York. During high school, she attended the American Academy of Dramatic Arts followed, during her sophomore year in college, by six months at the Gene Frankel Theater Workshop. Jan, who studied mime with Paul Curtis, graduated from Hofstra University with a BA in fine arts. During her twenties, she was a freelance theater critic for *Backstage* newspaper for seven years.

Jan went on to get a master's in criminal justice from Goddard College and a Ph.D. in sociology from the City University of New York Graduate Center. She also did a year of graduate work in art therapy at Hahnemann Medical College.

She is the author of 50+ award-winning nonfiction and fiction titles, translated into 35 languages, including the nonfiction books *When*

Friendship Hurts; Friendgevity; How to Finish Everything You Start; Essentials of Victimology; Victims; 365 Daily Affirmations for Happiness; Friendshifts; Looking Backward, Going Forward: Reflections on a Writer's Life; and four novels— *Untimely Death, Just Your Everyday People, The Pretty One*, and *On the Run*.

Over the years, Jan has taught undergraduate and graduate courses in sociology, criminology, victimology, writing, and public speaking. Since 2914, Jan has been teaching in the Sociology Department of John Jay College of Criminal Justice, where she is an award-winning Adjunct Associate Professor.

Jan is a member of several professional associations including The Dramatist Guild, The Authors Guild, and Womens Media Group. For more on Jan, visit her main website: https://www.drjanyager.com

**Books By Jan Yager You Might Find of
Interest**

NOVELS

The Pretty One
On the Run

(with Fred Yager)
Untimely Death
Just Your Everyday People

NONFICTION

On Friendship

Celebrating Friends and Friendship

Friendgevity

When Friendships Hurts

Friendshifts

On Family, Romance, Work Relationships

*365 Daily Affirmations for Healthy &
Nurturing Relationships*

125 Ways to Meet the Love of Your Life

On Work Relationships

Productive Relationships

*Who's That Sitting at My Desk? Workship,
Friendship, or Foe?*

On Speaking

The Fast Track Guide to Speaking in Public

On Crime and Crime Victims

Victims (Second edition)

Essentials of Victimology (Second edition)

On Money

21 Ways to Financial Freedom

On Productivity and Time Management

How to Finish Everything Your Start

Work Less, Do More: The 7-Day Productivity

Makeover Put More Time on Your Side

Creative Time Management for the New Millennium

Creative Time Management

Delivering Time Management for IT

Professionals: A Trainer's Manual

Making Your Office Work For You

The Fast Track Guide to Losing Weight and Keeping It Off

On Where to Get Help

Help Yourself Now: A Practical Guide to Finding the Information and Assistance You Need

Children's books

(3 books Illustrated by Mitzi Lyman)

The Cantaloupe Cat

The Reading Rabbit

The Quiet Dog

Fairy Tale Sequels, Book 1,

Little Red Riding Hood

Fairy Tale Sequels, Book 2,

The Three Little Pigs